This book belongs to

Characters (in order of appearance)
Narrator/Rafiki ROBERT GUILLAME
Young Simba   JONATHAM TAYLOS THOMAS
Young Nala   NAKITA CLAME
Mufasa   JAMES EARL JONES
Scar   JEREMY IRONS
Pumbaa   ERNIE SABELLA
Timon   NATHAN LANE
Shenzi   WHOOPI GOLDBERG
Banzai   CHEECH MARIN
Ed JIN   CUMMINGS
Sarabi   MADGE SINCLAIR
Simba   MATTHEW BRODERICK
Nala   MOIRA KELLY

Produced by RANDY THORNTON and TED KRYCZKO
Background score by HANS ZIMMER
Executive Producer GEORGE MORENCY
Adapted by JANE SCHONBERGER
Illustrated by The Walt Disney Studio

I Just Can't Wait to Be King (02.49)
Words by TIM RICE and Music by ELTON JOHN
Performed by JASON WEAVER, ROWAN ATKINSON and
LAURA WILLIAMS
Arranged and Produced by MARK MANCINA
© 1994 Walt Disney Music Company (ASCAP)/
Wonderland Music Company, Inc. (BMI).
All rights reserved.
℗ Walt Disney Records. © Disney. All rights reserved.
Under exclusive license to WEA International Inc.

This is a Parragon book
First published in 2006
Parragon
Queen Street House
4 Queen Street
Bath, BA1 1HE, UK

ISBN 1-40546-699-5
Manufactured in China

LION KING

p

Every morning, as the sun peeks over the horizon, a giant rock formation catches the first rays of light. This is Pride Rock, home to my good friend King Mufasa and his lovely wife, Queen Sarabi. On this particular morning, animals from all over the pride Lands had journeyed to Pride Rock to honour the birth of their newborn cub, Simba.

As part of the celebration, I had a special duty. I cracked open a gourd, dipped my finger inside, and made a mark on Simba's forehead. Then I lifted the future king up high for all to see. The elephants trumpeted with their trunks, the monkeys jumped up and down, and the zebras stamped their hooves with happiness.

Not far from the ceremony, in a cave at the back side of Pride Rock, a scraggly lion with a dark mane grumbled, "Life's not fair. I shall never be King." This was Mufasa's brother, Scar, who was jealous of Simba's position as the next king.

Moments later, Mufasa was at the doorway to the cave. "Sarabi and I didn't see you at the presentation of Simba."

Zazu, Mufasa's trusted advisor, also appeared. "You should have been first in line."

"I was first in line until the little hairball was born." And with that, Scar stalked out of the cave.

Before long, Simba grew into a healthy, playful young cub. Early one morning, he and Mufasa climbed to the top of Pride Rock. As they looked out at the rising sun, Mufasa pointed to the light beams that stretched across the Pride Lands. "Look, Simba: Everything the light touches is our kingdom."

Simba scanned the horizon and noticed a dark spot in the distance. "What about that shadowy place?"

"That's beyond our borders. You must never go there, Simba."

"But I thought a king can do whatever he wants."

"There's more to being a king than getting your way all the time. Everything you see exists together in a delicate balance. As King you need to understand that balance, and respect all the creatures – from the crawling ant to the leaping antelope. We are all connected in the great Circle of Life."

Later, as Simba headed back down the path, he ran into Scar. "Hey, Uncle Scar! Guess what? I'm gonna be King of Pride Rock. My dad just showed me the whole kingdom! And I'm gonna rule it all!"

Scar looked slyly at the young cub. "He didn't show you what's beyond that rise at the northern border."

"Well, no. He said I can't go there."

"And he's absolutely right. It's far too dangerous. Only the bravest lions go there. Promise me you'll never visit that dreadful place."

When Simba returned home, he found his friend Nala and her mother, Sarafina, visiting with Sarabi. "Come on! I just heard about this great place!"

The mothers gave permission for the youngsters to go, as long as Zazu went with them. Simba and Nala raced across the Pride Lands in an effort to lose the watchful bird. They led him through many herds of animals until they finally lost him.

Once the cubs were free of Zazu, Simba pounced on Nala, then Nala flipped Simba onto his back. They tumbled down a hill and landed in a dark ravine-littered with elephant skulls and bones.

Simba looked around and gasped. "This is it! We made it!"

Before the cubs could explore any farther, Zazu tracked them down.

"We're way beyond the boundary of the Pride Lands. And right now we are all in very real danger."

Suddenly, three hyenas slithered out the eye sockets of an elephant skull. Frightened, Simba, Zazu, and Nala jumped back. It was Banzai, his partner Shenzi, and the always-laughing Ed.

Banzai sneered. "A trio of trespassers."

Zazu tried to lead the cubs to safety, but Banzai grabbed him by the neck and plopped him down. The hyenas circled their prey, licking their chops.

"What's the hurry? We'd love you to stick around for dinner."

While the hyenas argued about who was going to eat
whom, Simba, Nala, and Zazu quietly slipped away. But
the hyenas weren't distracted for long. They gave chase,
and Simba and Nala had to run fast as they could.
Finally, they tried hiding behind some
elephant bones.

Just when it looked
as if it were all over
for the young cubs,
Mufasa appeared
and sent the hyenas
flying with a swipe
of his big paw.

"If you ever come near my son again…"
The hyenas slinked away, and Mufasa glared at Simba.
"You deliberately disobeyed me! I'm very disappointed
in you!"

Mufasa sent Nala and Zazu home so he could talk privately to his son. Simba peered up at his father.

"I was just trying to be brave, like you."

"Being brave doesn't mean you go looking for trouble."

"Dad, we're pals, right? And we'll always be together, right?"

Mufasa looked up and the stars. "Simba, let me tell you something my father told me: Look at the stars. The great kings of the past look down on us from those stars. So whenever you feel alone, just remember that those kings will always be there to guide you. And so will I."

Meanwhile, the hyenas received another visitor: an angry Scar showed up at their lair. "I practically gift-wrapped those cubs and you couldn't even dispose of them," Scar warned the hyenas to be prepared.

Banzai laughed. "Yeah! Be prepared. We'll be prepared! For what?"

Scar looked at him with danger in his eyes. "For the death of the king."

The following day, Scar invited Simba to join him in the gorge. When they arrived, Scar turned to his young nephew. "Now you wait here. Your father has a marvellous surprise for you."

Moments after he left, Scar signalled the hyenas, who chased a herd of wildebeests directly towards Simba.

From a distance, Mufasa noticed the rising dust. Scar appeared quickly at his side. "Stampede! In the gorge! Simba's down there!"

Without waiting a second, Mufasa took off to save his young son.

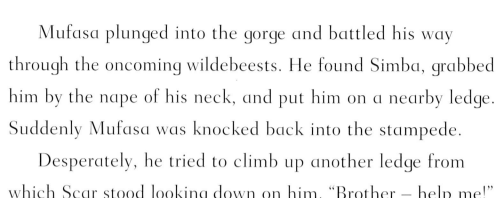

Mufasa plunged into the gorge and battled his way through the oncoming wildebeests. He found Simba, grabbed him by the nape of his neck, and put him on a nearby ledge. Suddenly Mufasa was knocked back into the stampede.

Desperately, he tried to climb up another ledge from which Scar stood looking down on him. "Brother – help me!"

Scar reached for Mufasa and pulled him close enough to whisper to his ear. "Long live the king." Then Scar let go of Mufasa and he fell to his death.

Simba peered over the ridge just as his father disappeared beneath the thundering stampede.

Later, Scar found Simba hovering over his father's body, sobbing. "It was an accident. I didn't mean for it to happen."

"But the king is dead. And if it weren't for you, he'd still be alive. Ah, what will your mother think?"

Simba sobbed harder. "What am I going to do?"

"Run away, Simba. Run! Run away and never return."

Simba did as he was told, unaware that his uncle's hyena friends had been ordered to finish him off. Scar returned to Pride Rock to take over the throne.

Meanwhile, Simba plodded across the savannah without any food or water. It wasn't long before he fainted under the hot sun.

As the vultures circled overhead, a big-hearted warthog named Pumbaa stumbled upon the young lion. He turned to his trusty pal, a fast-talking meerkat named Timon. "He's so cute and all alone. Can we keep him?"

"Pumbaa, are you nuts? Lions eat guys like us." But Pumbaa scooped Simba up anyway, and carried him to safety.

When Simba awoke, the first thought that sprang to his mind was his father's death. Timon taught him about Hakuna Matata, which means no responsibilities, no worries.

"You've got to put your past behind you."

And that is exactly what Simba did. He stayed in the jungle with Pumbaa and Timon a long, long time, and grew into a very big lion. But eventually he got homesick. One night he looked up at the stars and recalled the words his father had told him long ago. "The great kings of the past look down on us from those stars. So whenever you feel alone, just remember that those kings will always be there to guide you. And so will I."

The next day, Pumbaa was stalked and chased by a lioness. Simba came to his rescue, but after wrestling with the lioness, who easily flipped him onto his back, he realised that she was his old friend.

"Nala? What are you doing here?"

"Why didn't you come back to Pride Rock? You're the king!"

"I'm not the king. Scar is."

"Simba, he let the hyenas take over the Pride Lands."

"What?"

"There's no food, no water. If you don't do something soon, everyone will starve. You're our only hope."

"I can't go back."

Simba yelled at the heavens. "You said you'd always be there for me, but you're not – because of me."

Simba didn't believe he could challenge Scar to the throne, so he stayed in the jungle with Nala and his new friends.

But I knew the time had come for Simba to take his place in the Circle of Life, and I headed for the jungle.

When Simba saw me, he was surprised. "Who are you?"

"The question is: Who are you?"

"I thought I knew. Now I'm not so sure."

"Well, I know who you are. You're Mufasa's boy. He's alive, and I'll show him to you. You follow old Rafiki. He knows the way."

I led Simba to a reflecting pool. When he looked into the water, he saw a lion. "That not my father. It's just my reflection."

"Look harder... You see, he lives in you."

The ghost of Mufasa magically appeared. "Look inside yourself, Simba. You are more than what you have become. You must take your place in the Circle of Life."

Encouraged by his father's words, Simba returned to Pride Rock. Nala, Pumbaa, and Timon followed. When Simba arrived, he found the land bare and dry. The hyenas were in control, and Scar was shouting at Simba's mother. Sarabi turned to Scar. "We must leave Pride Rock."

"We're not going anywhere. I am the king."

"You are half the king Mufasa was –"

"I AM TEN TIMES THE KING MUFASA WAS!"

Suddenly, a flash of lightning revealed the edge of Pride Rock, and there stood Simba. Scar jumped back.

"Simba… I'm a little surprised to see you… alive."

"Give me one good reason why I shouldn't rip you apart."

But Scar forced Simba to say, in front of all the lions, that he had caused his father's death.

Scar smirked. "Oh Simba, you're in trouble again. But this time Daddy isn't here to save you. And now everybody knows why."

Simba backed up against the ledge.
Lightning struck again, setting fire
to the dry brush of the Pride Lands.
Simba, knowing the truth, leapt
on Scar. Nala and the other lionesses
joined the battle. Through the smoke
and flames of the bushfire, Simba
spotted Scar trying to escape and he
ran after the old lion. Scar pleaded with
his nephew.

"Simba, I'll make it up to you. I promise.
How can I prove myself to you?"

"Run. Run away, Scar and never return."

Scar started to slink off, but then he turned and
lunged one last time at Simba. Simba moved quickly
and flipped Scar over the ledge, where a pack of hyenas
were waiting hungrily.

Limping badly, Simba climbed up to the very top of Pride Rock. He let out a magnificent roar as he looked out over his kingdom.

Before long, Pride Rock flourished again. Nala remained by Simba's side, and soon they had their own newborn cub. With all their friends around, including Zazu, Pumbaa, and Timon, a new celebration of life took place. After making a mark on the forehead of the young cub, I held him up for all the kingdom to see.

Now you have finished reading the story
of Lion King, why not sing along
with this magical song from the movie?

I JUST CAN'T WAIT TO BE KING

Music by Elton John. Lyrics by Tim Rice

Performed by Jason Weaver, Rowan Atkinson and Laura Williams

Arranged and produced by Mark Mancina

I'm gonna be a mighty king
So enemies beware!
Well, I've never seen a king of beasts
With quite so little hair

I'm gonna be the mane event
Like no king was before
I'm brushing up on looking down
I'm working on my roar

Thus far, a rather uninspiring thing
Oh, I just can't wait to be king!
You've rather a long way to go,
Young master, if you think...

No one saying do this
Now, when I said that I...
No one saying be there
What I meant was...
No one saying stop that
Look, what you don't realize...
No one saying see here
Now see here!
Free to run around all day
Well that's definitely
out of the...
Free to do it all my way

I think it's time that you and I
Arranged a heart to heart
Kings don't need advice
From little hornbills for a start

If this is where the monarchy is headed
Count me out
Out of service, out of Africa
I wouldn't hang about
This child is getting wildly out of wing

Oh, I just can't wait to be king!

Everybody look left
Everybody look right
Everywhere you look I'm
Standing in the spotlight
          Not yet...

Let every creature go for broke and sing
Let's hear it in the herd and on the wing
It's gonna be King Simba's finest fling

Oh, I just can't wait to be king!
Oh, I just can't wait to be king!
Oh, I just can't wait to be king!